The Tiara Club

For all the wonderful
princesses and princes I met in Malta,
with lots of love xxx
VF
With very special thanks to JD

www.tiaraclub.co.uk

ORCHARD BOOKS
338 Euston Road, London NW1 3BH
Orchard Books Australia
Level 17/207 Kent St, Sydney, NSW 2000

A Paperback Original
First published in Great Britain in 2009
Text © Vivian French 2009
Illustrations © Orchard Books 2009

The right of Vivian French to be identified as the author of this
work has been asserted by her in accordance with the Copyright,
Designs and Patents Act 1988.

A CIP catalogue record for this book is available
from the British Library.

ISBN 978 1 40830 579 9

1 3 5 7 9 10 8 6 4 2

Printed in Great Britain

Orchard Books is a division of Hachette Children's Books,
an Hachette UK company
www.hachette.co.uk

Rose Petal Picnic

with Princess Anna and Princess Elizabeth

By Vivian French

ORCHARD BOOKS

The Royal Palace Academy
for the Preparation of Perfect Princesses

(Known to our students as "*The Princess Academy*")

OUR SCHOOL MOTTO:

*A Perfect Princess always thinks of others
before herself, and is kind, caring and truthful.*

**Diamond Turrets offers a complete education for
Tiara Club princesses, focusing on caring for animals
and the environment. The curriculum includes:**

*A visit to the Royal
County Show*

*Visits to the Country
Park and Bamboo Grove*

*Work experience on our
very own farm*

*Elephant rides in our
Safari Park (students
will be closely supervised)*

**Our headteacher, King Percy, is present at all times, and
students are well looked after by Fairy G, the school
Fairy Godmother.**

Our resident staff and visiting experts include:

LADY WHITSTABLE-KENT
(IN CHARGE OF THE FARM,
COUNTRY PARK AND SAFARI PARK)

FAIRY ANGORA
(ASSISTANT FAIRY GODMOTHER)

FARMER KATE
(DOMESTIC ANIMALS)

QUEEN MOTHER MATILDA
(ETIQUETTE, POSTURE AND
APPEARANCE)

LADY MAY (SUPERVISOR OF THE
HOLIDAY HOME FOR PETS)

We award tiara points to encourage our Tiara Club princesses towards the next level. All princesses who win enough points at Diamond Turrets will be presented with their Diamond Sashes and attend a celebration ball.

Diamond Sash Tiara Club princesses are invited to return to Golden Gates, our magnificent mansion residence for Perfect Princesses, where they may continue their education at a higher level.

PLEASE NOTE:
Princesses are expected to arrive at
the Academy with a *minimum* of:

TWENTY BALLGOWNS
(with all necessary hoops,
petticoats, etc)

TWELVE DAY DRESSES

SEVEN GOWNS
suitable for garden parties
and other special
day occasions

TWELVE TIARAS

DANCING SHOES
five pairs

VELVET SLIPPERS
three pairs

RIDING BOOTS
two pairs

Wellington boots, waterproof
cloaks and other essential
protective clothing
as required

Hi! I'm Princess Anna - PLEASE
don't muddle me up with Princess
Elizabeth, my twin sister. We're very
different - honestly! Elizabeth was
really worried about going to Diamond
Turrets, but I couldn't wait to get there.
'Stop fussing!' I told her. 'It'll be
FABULOUS!' But that was before
I found out about the other twins,
horrible Diamonde and Gruella...

Chapter One

When Mum told me we were going to Diamond Turrets I nearly burst with excitement. Our uncle, King Percy, is the head teacher there, and it sounded such fun! There's a farm, and gardens, and a safari park, and all kinds of different animals. My twin sister, Elizabeth, wasn't pleased at all, though.

She's SO not like me – she's really shy. She told Mum she didn't want to go, but Mum just gave her a hug.

"You'll have a lovely time," she said, "and Uncle Percy will keep an eye on you."

Elizabeth looked very worried. "PLEASE don't make me go!"

"I'm afraid it's all arranged, darling," Mum told her. "I'm going to stay with Grandmother until she's feeling better, and I can't leave you here on your own."

Elizabeth gulped and ran out of the throne room. I went to find her, and she was lying on her bed clutching a wet hankie. "It'll be OK," I said. "I'll look after you."

Elizabeth sniffed very loudly. "Promise, Anna," she said, and I promised.

Uncle Percy was taking us to Diamond Turrets in his carriage, and he arrived REALLY early.

"Hope you don't mind," he said, "but I've got a lot of work to do."

Elizabeth was looking worried again. "Will the other princesses tease us because you're our uncle?"

Uncle Percy laughed. "Don't call me Uncle P, and they'll never know!"

That made Elizabeth smile, and we spent the rest of the journey practising calling him "King Percy". It seemed no time at all until we were trotting through some tall gates, and Uncle – I mean, King – Percy announced, "We're here!"

Have you ever been in a school when nobody else was around? It felt SO strange! But King Percy introduced us to the school fairy godmother, Fairy G, and she was lovely – although she didn't look a bit like a fairy. She had big boots, and a really loud voice.

"Delighted to see you both!" she boomed. "You'll be sleeping in Tulip Room, my dears, but no need to unpack just yet. Go and have a look round outside – it's a lovely day!"

We thanked her, and walked out into the sunshine. We found the farm, and said hello to the animals, and then we went to see what was on the other side of a tall iron gate. Elizabeth gave a happy squeak. "OH! It's the most beautiful rose garden!"

She was right; it was really beautiful. There were pretty roses everywhere, and the scent was heavenly. We wandered round for ages, and we were just wondering if we should go back when we saw two princesses walking towards us – and we could tell just by looking at them that they were twins as well!

"Hi," I said cheerfully. "We're new here. I'm Anna, and this is Elizabeth."

The twins didn't answer. They just stood and stared at us. Then one said, "Nobody told us you were coming. Did they, Gruella?"

"No, Diamonde, they didn't." Gruella sounded just as snooty as her sister. "What room are you in?"

"Tulip Room," I said. A horrible thought struck me, and I asked, "Are you in Tulip Room too?"

Diamonde looked down her nose at me. "WE have our own room. Mummy didn't want us to share with a whole lot of ordinary princesses."

I was beginning to get cross. "I'm an ordinary princess, and so is Elizabeth, and there's absolutely nothing wrong with anyone being ordinary!"

Diamonde shrugged. "If you say so. Come on, Gruella. Let's go and pick some roses for our room." And she grabbed her sister's arm and flounced away.

"Phew!" I said. "Weren't they simply dreadful?"

Elizabeth shuddered. "Dreadful. I do hope the others aren't like that!" Then she pointed. "Look! There's the dearest little summer house over there, and it's COVERED in roses!"

We went to sit inside, and it was SO lovely. Elizabeth shut her eyes. "This is BLISS," she said. "Roses really and truly are my most favourite flowers ever."

They certainly were. Once she collected loads of rose petals and she and Cook spent hours making rose petal jelly – it was delicious! And she's made sugared rose petals, and even rose-scented ice cream! Elizabeth may be shy, but she's brilliant at cooking all sorts of things.

All of a sudden we sat up straight. There were footsteps behind the summer house, and a familiar voice.

"Honestly, Gruella! Weren't they RUDE?"

"But they're not as pretty as us, Diamonde." Gruella sounded very pleased with herself.

Diamonde sniffed. "I wonder where they went? Come on, Gruella. I've had a brilliant idea. Let's make sure everyone in Tulip Room just LOVES the new twins!"

Chapter Two

As the footsteps died away Elizabeth looked anxious. "What did they mean?" she asked.

"I don't know," I said, "but I don't want to meet them again until we have to. Why don't we wait a few minutes until they've gone?"

My twin thought that was

a good idea, so we sat on in the summer house for a while before having another potter round the garden. Elizabeth found a climbing rose covered in tiny pink buds, and she picked a little bunch. "Look!" she said. "They're so lovely! We could put them in our room."

We must have been outside a long time, because when we got back Diamond Turrets was buzzing! Pages were hurrying to and fro carrying trunks in from a row of carriages, and loads of princesses were saying goodbye to their friends and relations. As we walked towards the door a really pretty princess whizzed up in her wheelchair, waving madly.

"Hi! You must be Anna and Elizabeth! I'm Lindsey, and Fairy G. asked me to look out for you."

You know when you meet someone and you just know for certain that you're going to be friends? Well, that's how I felt then, and I know Elizabeth did too.

"I'll show you round," Lindsey went on, "and then I'll take you to the recreation room. The others from Tulip Room are longing to meet you!"

"Oh." I suddenly remembered

the twins in the rose garden. "Erm...has a princess called Diamonde said anything to you about us?"

Lindsey looked very surprised. "Diamonde? No. Why?"

I hesitated. "Oh...we met her and her sister earlier."

"H'm." Lindsey gave me a sideways look. "What did they say to you?"

A Perfect Princess doesn't tell tales, so I just said, "Oh...nothing much."

We followed Lindsey as she led us along the corridors and showed us where the hall was, and the ballroom, and the classrooms. Finally she took us to the dormitories and, when she opened the door to Tulip Room, it was SO pretty I couldn't stop smiling. There were tulip shaped bedside lamps and the softest carpet, and almost everything was patterned with tulips or tulip leaves.

"It's GORGEOUS!" I said. "Do you know which beds are ours, Lindsey?"

Lindsey took us to the end of the room. "Can you help me open these?" she asked, and pointed to two big double doors. Elizabeth and I pushed, and Lindsey pulled, and the doors folded neatly back against the wall...and we saw two cosy beds, with our trunks stacked beside them.

"It's the Tulip Room annexe,"

Lindsey explained, "but it'll be much more fun if we keep the doors open so we can all be together. Is that all right with you?"

"It certainly is!" I said, and Elizabeth nodded. She put her bunch of rosebuds in a glass on her bedside table, and Lindsey grinned.

"Those look lovely! Have you been in the rose garden?"

Elizabeth nodded again, but before she had time to answer a loud bell began to ring.

"Ooops!" Lindsey swung her wheelchair round. "That's the warning bell for assembly. Abigail says King Percy's going to make a special announcement – we're SO excited! I'll go and save you places in the hall." And then she was gone.

Chapter Three

Elizabeth and I washed our hands and brushed our hair, then made our way to the hall. There were SO many princesses! Luckily we saw Lindsey before Elizabeth could get anxious, and I knew the princesses sitting with her must be her friends. They looked very different from Diamonde and

Gruella, and they smiled at us as we sat down.

Lindsey introduced us. "Caitlin, Bethany, Abigail, Rebecca and Mia – meet Elizabeth and Anna!"

"No talking at the back!" A tall, horsey-looking woman had stepped out onto the stage, and was glaring at us. Elizabeth went pale, but Bethany winked at her.

"That's Lady Whitstable-Kent," she whispered. "Don't let her scare you! She's OK really."

And then our uncle strode out, and I almost didn't recognise him. He looked hugely important in his cloak and his crown. Beside him was Fairy G, and a truly beautiful fairy in the most glorious sparkly blue-green dress.

"Good afternoon, princesses,

and may I welcome you to a new term at Diamond Turrets!" King Percy sounded very grand. "Now, I have a surprise for you. Our assistant fairy godmother, Fairy Angora—" (the beautiful fairy blushed) "has been awarded her Final Certificate by the College of Fairy Godmothers! We are all absolutely delighted, and I hope you will join me in offering her our heartiest congratulations." He bowed to Fairy Angora, and we all clapped madly. Fairy Angora blushed some more, then curtsied before moving to the front of the stage.

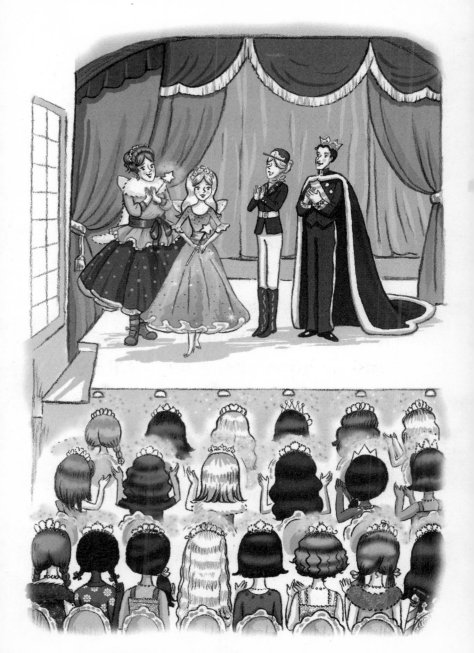

"Dear princesses," she said, and her voice was very sweet and silvery. "All of you have helped me so much. My certificate will be presented by the President of the Association of Fairy Godmothers, our very own Fairy G. And King Percy has a truly wonderful idea. He suggests the presentation takes place here at Diamond Turrets – and we all celebrate with a Rose Petal Picnic!"

You should have heard the noise! Of course Perfect Princesses don't shout and stamp their feet, but they can laugh and cheer and clap. It wasn't until Fairy G waved her wand that we were silent.

"We'll have the presentation in the rose garden," she boomed, "and we'll be asking you for ideas to make it a VERY special day.

And one last thing. The princesses who have the best ideas will be Fairy Angora's flower girls when the certificate is presented."

This time there was a stunned silence until Diamonde put her hand up. "I expect Gruella and I will win," she said, "because Mummy says we have the BEST ideas, but do you mean ideas about games to play or decorations?"

There was definitely a chilly note in Fairy G's voice as she answered.

"We don't wish to ask for specific ideas, Diamonde. We want you to think about Fairy Angora and how you can make the Rose Petal Picnic one of her happiest memories. Now, there are no lessons today, so you can start thinking straightaway – and you can work in pairs, or in groups. Make sure you put your names on your papers, and I'll collect the ideas after break tomorrow."

Diamonde didn't quite say,

"H'mph!" but she flumped back into her seat.

Rebecca shook her head as we waited to leave the hall. "Have you met Diamonde and Gruella? They're AWFUL."

Mia sighed. "They're always causing trouble. Hey – did you see those scratches on Diamonde's hand? What's she been doing?"

"I saw her in the garden," I said. "Maybe she was picking roses."

Bethany shook her head. "Fairy G waved her wand and took all the thorns away. Only the main stalks have thorns on them."

"Don't worry about her," Mia interrupted. "Now, has anyone any ideas?"

And then I had the shock of my life. My twin, Elizabeth, my shy little sister, actually spoke.

"Maybe," she said, "we could plan a rose petal menu for the picnic?" She hesitated, then went on. "There are lots and LOTS of roses in the garden, and we could make rose petal jelly and ice cream..."

"WOW!" The Tulip Room princesses stared at her.

"That's INCREDIBLE!" Abigail breathed. "Can you actually make those things?"

Elizabeth nodded, and I said, "She's a brilliant cook. She made rose petal and violet chocolate creams for our mother's birthday, and everyone said they were completely delicious!"

Bethany put her head on one side. "Maybe we could dream up some other ideas, and Elizabeth can tell us if she thinks they'd work."

"Let's go." Rebecca linked her arm through Elizabeth's. "Tell me about those chocolate creams. They sound FABULOUS..."

Chapter Four

We had such fun that afternoon. We planned all kinds of rose petal treats, including rose flavoured lemonade! By supper time it felt as if we'd known each other for ever, and even Elizabeth chatted away without any of her usual silences. When the bell went for bed we were fizzing with excitement.

I was just about to write Caitlin's suggestion for "Rose-scented candles" on our list, when Princess Charlotte came to find me.

"Please could you and your sister come to Fairy G's study?" she asked. "She wants to make sure you're settling in OK."

We waved to the others and followed Charlotte. She left us outside the study door, and we knocked and went in. Fairy G wasn't there, though. It was Uncle Percy, and he laughed when he saw our astonished faces.

"I thought it would be less suspicious if I met you here," he said. "Tell me, how are you getting on?"

We couldn't stop talking. There were so many lovely things to tell him about, especially our new friends. Uncle P listened carefully, and when we finished he looked really pleased. "Excellent," he said.

"They're a splendid lot in Tulip Room. And now you'd better hurry off to bed. I don't want you to be tired for lessons tomorrow!"

We thanked him, and skipped off down the long corridor. As we reached the door of Tulip Room Elizabeth smiled the most lovely smile. "I NEVER EVER thought I'd like it here," she said, "but I do. I LOVE it!"

"Me too," I agreed, and flung open the door. "We're here!" I announced – and then I froze. Our new friends were lying in bed with their backs to us. They looked as if they were asleep, but I'm sure they were pretending. And the double doors at the end were shut, except for a crack just wide enough to let us through...

they didn't want us sharing their room with them.

When we tiptoed into our little annexe we saw a note pinned to my pillow.

Dear Princess Anna and
Princess Elizabeth,
Thank you for your help today. We enjoyed it. I'm afraid we don't like nasty practical jokes, though, so we've decided to try and think of some other ideas for the Rose Petal Picnic. We'll leave you the rose petal menu because it was your idea.
Yours sincerely,
Caitlin, Mia, Bethany, Abigail and Rebecca.

I stared and stared. Elizabeth sank onto her bed.

"I knew it was too good to last," she wailed. "I want to go home..." Big fat tears welled up in her eyes, and she threw herself onto her pillows. I watched her shoulders shaking, and tried to think what had gone wrong as I read and re-read the note. WHAT practical joke?

And then I noticed something. Lindsey hadn't signed her name! Did that mean she didn't agree with the others? I took a deep breath, and crept out between the two doors. Lindsey stirred as

I tiptoed up to her bed. "Lindsey," I whispered, "I'm sorry to wake you, but PLEASE tell me. What are we supposed to have done?" She didn't answer, and I took a step nearer...

...and YELLED! I'd trodden on something REALLY sharp, and as I hopped about on one foot everyone sat bolt upright in bed.

"Ow ow ow!" I collapsed onto the floor and pulled my foot towards me. There was a HUGE thorn in my foot, and as I pulled it out, I saw that there were two or three more on Lindsey's bedside rug.

"These are FEARSOME!" I gasped. "However did they get here?" Very carefully I felt about in the woolly rug until I was sure I'd found all the thorns, and held out my hand for Lindsey to see. She studied them for a moment, then folded her arms and positively glared at her friends.

"I TOLD you Anna and Elizabeth didn't do it!" She turned back to me. "Anna, I'm really sorry about this. There were thorns like those in everybody's rugs and, as you'd been in the rose garden earlier today, the others thought it must have been you.

And I did leave you here on your
own when I went down for
assembly."

Caitlin shook her head. "We're
all SO stupid. You'd never have
stepped on them if you'd been the
one to put them there."

I didn't know what to say. I'd NEVER play a trick like that – not even on someone I didn't like.

"I've just thought of something," Mia said thoughtfully. "Diamonde had all those scratches... Do you think she and Gruella did it?"

Rebecca came to sit on the edge of Lindsey's bed. "But why? Why would they want to make us think Anna and Elizabeth are horrible?"

"I've got an idea about that," Lindsey said quietly. "I think Anna might have upset them by accident." She patted my hand. "You said you met them in the garden, but you didn't tell me what they said. Did they say something mean? Did you fall out with them?"

I fiddled with the edge of the blanket. I did NOT want to be a tell-tale, but I did give a little nod. Lindsey gave a pleased grunt. "I thought so."

"I feel terrible," Bethany said. "Anna – what can we do to make it up to you?"

I looked at the closed doors at the end of the room. "Could we open the doors again?"

So we opened the doors, and Elizabeth gave such a loud squeak of surprise we couldn't help laughing. A moment later there was a loud knock on the door, and Fairy G came striding in.

"What IS this noise about?" she demanded. "You should all be asleep! I want some excellent ideas tomorrow, remember."

"We've had the BEST ideas," Abigail told her. "At least, Elizabeth has!"

"Don't say another word," Fairy G told her. "Now – everyone in bed before I count to three, One...two...three!" And then she waved her wand...

The next thing I knew I was waking up to the brightest summery morning ever.

Chapter Five

We could hardly wait until the lesson after break. Fairy G went round collecting up all the suggestions for the Rose Petal Picnic. She stopped to read each one as she was given it, and we nearly burst because we were last. It was worth waiting, though. When she saw what we'd written she beamed and BEAMED at us.

"Well done, Tulip Room! All the other suggestions are to do with rose ribbons and decorations, or pink velvet and satin dresses."

Diamonde jumped to her feet and waved her hand in the air.

"Fairy G! Fairy G! WE had a BRILLIANT idea! We thought of rose-tinted spectacles so everyone would look prettier!"

Fairy G frowned. "Really, Diamonde..." she paused, and took Diamonde's hands in hers. Diamonde snatched them away and hid them behind her back, and as she did so I saw her look at me with SUCH a horrible expression I knew for certain she'd put the thorns in Tulip Room.

"ROSE scratches, Diamonde?" Fairy G's eyebrows rose. "May I ask WHY your hands are covered in scratches? I took care to remove all the thorns from around the flowers…"

"But we wanted…" Gruella began, then saw Diamonde's face, and blushed so red she almost glowed.

Diamonde did her best to smile, but it was obviously false. "I just…that is, I just slipped. Didn't I, Gruella?"

"Oh yes," Gruella agreed brightly. "She slipped."

Fairy G looked round at the rest of us. "Have any of you anything to say?"

Of course we didn't say a word,

but Fairy G gave the twins a very steely stare before she turned back to the pile of papers. "As I was saying, Tulip Room have come up with a delightfully original idea. Well done!"

Mia pushed Elizabeth forward. "It was Elizabeth," she explained, "We just helped."

"I'll check with all the other classes," Fairy G said, "but I think I can say there's no doubt about it. Mmmm...rose petal chocolate creams. My favourite!" And she was humming as she stomped out of the door.

We looked at each other, eyes shining. "Does that mean we get to be flower girls at the presentation?" I whispered.

"I think it does," Lindsey said, and we all hugged Elizabeth until she complained she couldn't breathe any more.

Chapter Six

We were right. When King Percy stood up in assembly the next day he announced we were the winners...and we couldn't help jumping up and down. I think we might even have stamped – just a little! We were going to be Fairy Angora's flower girls at the Rose Petal Picnic presentation!

And that night when we were getting ready for bed we talked for ages and ages.

"Do you think Fairy G knows what Diamonde and Gruella did?" Mia asked sleepily.

"I'm sure she knows they did something," Abigail said. "But they didn't get what they wanted, did they? Anna and Elizabeth are our special friends for ever and ever..."

I saw the blissful smile on Elizabeth's face, and I knew I looked exactly the same. That's one of the fun things about being a twin!

And do you know what?

You're our special friend as well...for ever and ever.

Hello. Have you met Anna,
my twin sister? If you have, you'll know
I'm horribly shy...I really am.
But I'm very lucky, because I'm friends
with all the princesses in Tulip Room –
that's Caitlin, Mia, Rebecca, Lindsey,
Abigail and Bethany. I don't even
mind too much about the horrid twins,
Diamonde and Gruella. We don't
let them spoil our fun.
And – did you know?
We're going to be flower girls when
Fairy Angora gets her Final Certificate
at the Rose Petal Picnic!

Chapter One

I was SO nervous before the Rose Petal Picnic. Anna kept telling me not to worry, but if you're like me you'll know that doesn't help. My stomach felt as if it was full of butterflies nearly all the time.

I was nervous because Tulip Room had made up the menu for the picnic, and lots of the suggestions were mine. I kept wondering what I would do if anything went wrong. It would be absolutely TERRIBLE if I spoiled Fairy Angora's special day! Fairy G was going to present the Final Certificate from the College of Fairy Godmothers to Fairy Angora, and then there was going to be a wonderful celebration. Mia told me there was even going to be dancing – but I knew nobody would enjoy it if the food was horrible.

I had another worry as well. Every time I saw Diamonde or Gruella they sneered at me.

"Oooooh! It's little cookie clever clogs! Aren't you going to make a rosie posie cake, then?"

I told them over and over again that I wasn't going to make a cake, but I can't be fierce like Anna, and I couldn't make them stop. But then I had an idea in the middle of the night – maybe I SHOULD make a cake?

I waited until breakfast the next morning, and then I asked Anna and the rest of Tulip Room what they thought.

"YES!" Bethany's eyes sparkled. "You could make it as a surprise."

"You could make it look like her certificate," Lindsey suggested.

Abigail waved her toast in the air. "A scroll, with lots of rose petals!"

"Hang on a minute." Caitlin was frowning. "What if the certificate is only a piece of paper?"

"Let's go and ask Fairy G!" Mia and Rebecca said together, and that's what we did. As soon as breakfast was over we hurried to Fairy G's study.

"Excuse me," Mia said, "but Elizabeth is going to make Fairy Angora a cake, and we thought it would be fun if it looked like her certificate. Could you tell us if it's a scroll or a piece of paper?"

Fairy G gave us a thoughtful look, and then she asked if we could keep a secret. Of course we said we could, and she went to one of her many cupboards and brought out the most impressive looking scroll. It was covered in heavy wax seals and had rose-coloured tassels hanging off the end.

"This," Fairy G told us, "is the

certificate I'll be giving Fairy Angora. But not a word!"

"Not a word," we agreed.

"You won't tell anyone about the cake, will you?" Anna asked. "We want it to be a surprise."

Fairy G nodded solemnly. "Let's all keep our secrets!"

When we'd thanked Fairy G, and said goodbye, we saw the other twins rushing towards us along the corridor.

"We've had a BRILLIANT idea for Fairy Angora's party." Gruella said, and she sounded very excited. "You said you're not making a cake, so we're going to, and it'll be a big surprise—"

"Sh!" Diamonde frowned at her sister as she knocked on Fairy G's door. "It's meant to be a secret!"

Fairy G boomed, "Come in!" and the twins hurried inside, slamming the door behind them.

"Oh no!" Rebecca stared after them. "Two surprise cakes. What do you think Fairy G will say?"

"I'm quite sure she'll think of something," Caitlin said. "Come on. We'd better hurry – cookery class starts in two minutes!"

Chapter Two

We made our way to the cookery room, and found Lady Victoria putting on her apron.

"Good morning, princesses. It's our special picnic very soon, so let's begin by making crystallised rose petals. Princess Elizabeth, would you be kind enough to write the recipe on the blackboard?"

I blushed pinker than the rose petals. I'd just started to write when Diamonde and Gruella came in, smiling from ear to ear.

"We're sorry we're late, Lady Victoria," they said together.

"We had something important to discuss with Fairy G," Diamonde explained. "We've had an AMAZING idea for the Rose Petal Picnic. We're going to make a special cake for Fairy Angora." She turned to look at all of us. "It's a secret, so we want you to promise not to tell anybody about it. Put up your hands if you promise!"

We all put up our hands, and Diamonde nodded. "Even Fairy G doesn't know what sort of cake we're making. It's going to be ENORMOUS, and when Fairy Angora cuts it open Gruella and

I will jump out and read a poem. It'll be SUCH a surprise!"

Lady Victoria considered the idea. "It'll need to be a very big cake to hide the two of you, Princess Diamonde. Wouldn't it be better if just one of you jumped out?"

"I will!" Diamonde said quickly.

Gruella glared at her. "But I want to!"

"NO!" Diamonde stamped her foot. "ME!"

Gruella folded her arms and stuck out her lower lip. "I'M going to jump out of the cake! YOU can read the poem!"

"PRINCESSES! Please!" Lady Victoria was horrified. "Take three minus tiara points! This is a cookery lesson, not a time for silly squabbles!"

The twins stormed off to their seats, and we went on with the lesson. I was worried that I had got the ingredients wrong...but luckily everything turned out well.

"Very good!" Lady Victoria stalked round inspecting our trays of sugar-covered rose petals.

"Those will be wonderful once they've dried. Five tiara points for every princess! Tomorrow we'll make rose-coloured lemonade." And then she strode out of the room.

Diamonde and Gruella went on arguing. It was mid-morning break, so we decided to leave them to it and go for a walk round the farm to see the darling piglets. We were just making our way out when we saw Fairy G stomping towards us.

"Tulip Room! Just the princesses I wanted to see!" She tucked her arm through mine, but she didn't say anything more until we were right outside. Then she stopped, and smiled at us. "I expect you're wondering why I said Diamonde and Gruella could make a cake when I knew you'd planned to make one." She gave the tiniest of

sighs. "They don't always think of others before themselves, I'm afraid, but they told me they really want to make Fairy Angora's day special, and I'd like to encourage them. So – I have a suggestion." Fairy G's eyes began to twinkle.

"The whole school will parade to the pavilion in the rose garden, and King Percy will make a speech of welcome. When that's over I'll present Fairy Angora with her certificate, and after that the twins can give her their cake. King Percy will invite everyone to the picnic, but I'll announce we have one last surprise. And THAT'S the moment when you, Elizabeth, will present your cake! How does that sound?"

I couldn't say a word. I could NEVER stand up in front of the whole school! Luckily Anna knew what I was thinking.

"Would it be all right if we all gave Fairy Angora the cake together?" she asked.

Fairy G nodded. "Of course. A cake from Tulip Room. Now, off you go. You don't want to be late for your next lesson!"

*

Once I knew I didn't have to do anything on my own I felt better. I almost enjoyed our lesson on "Visiting Scottish Royalty", even though the teacher was Queen Mother Matilda. She always makes me nervous because she's so strict. At the end she asked Tulip Room to stay behind, though, and the butterflies started whizzing round and round my stomach again.

"Tulip Room princesses!" Queen Mother Matilda barked. "You are to be Fairy Angora's flower girls, and King Percy has asked me to make the arrangements. I suggest you parade two by two; we will practise tonight. Each of you will have a basket of roses to carry.

When you reach the pavilion, before King Percy makes his speech, you will join Fairy Angora on stage, and shower her with rose petals." The queen allowed herself a little smile. "It will look delightful. Now, the Grand High Duchess Delia is waiting for you in the sewing room, so you'd better hurry."

Chapter Three

I don't think I'd realised we were going to have special dresses to wear. They were GORGEOUS! They were pink taffeta with pale pink net petticoats, and our shoes had tiny rosebuds on the toes. Duchess Delia nodded approvingly as we stood in a row for her to inspect us all.

"Very nice, princesses. You'll make perfect flower girls!"

We were just thanking her when the door opened and Diamonde and Gruella came flouncing in.

"I need a special dress, Duchess Delia," Gruella began.

Diamonde elbowed her way in front of her sister. "Gruella and I BOTH need something special to wear."

The duchess frowned. "I'm sorry, Princess Diamonde, but that won't be possible. I have to finish Fairy Angora's dress." She pointed to an absolutely GORGEOUS dress with wide hooped petticoats. It was a soft sky blue, and there was an enormous blue silk bow on the front.

Diamonde and Gruella stared, their eyes shining.

"That's simply WONDERFUL!" Gruella breathed.

"Come on, Gruella." Diamonde grabbed her twin's arm. "We want dresses exactly like that. Let's go and write to Mummy." And they flounced out again.

Duchess Delia shook her head.

"Dear me. Now, let's hang your dresses up. It's nearly time for lunch."

We waved her goodbye, and walked towards the dining room.

"When are you going to make the cake?" Abigail asked me as we went in.

"What about after school tomorrow?" I suggested, and we decided that would be perfect. But Queen Mother Matilda wanted us to rehearse again, and the day after that as well. The following day King Percy asked us all to go into the rose garden to help pick roses to decorate the pavilion, and I began to wonder if we'd EVER get the cake made.

On the other hand the picnic preparations were going really well. We'd made the rose-coloured lemonade in cookery, and rose-flavoured chocolate creams, as well as pink iced biscuits and rose petal jellies. Nothing had gone wrong, much to my relief, even though Diamonde and Gruella were REALLY annoying. They'd made their enormous cake, but they used ALL the crystallised rose petals to decorate it. The one good thing was that they weren't arguing any more. They'd decided Diamonde was going to jump out, and Gruella would read the poem.

"Fairy Angora will be SO surprised," Diamonde boasted. "I expect we'll get LOADS of tiara points."

*

We finally found time to go to the cookery room the evening before the day of the picnic, but things didn't go right. Lady Victoria stayed until we'd got the cake safely out of the oven and cool enough to work with, but then she had to go. I began to cut the cake into the right kind of shape, but however hard I tried I just couldn't make it look like a scroll.

"It's a disaster," I said as I stared at the horrible mess in front of me.

Abigail put her arm round me. "I'm sure it'll be fine once you've iced it."

Caitlin reached out and turned the cake board round. "Do you know," she said slowly, "I think you could make it look like a bow."

"Caitlin's quite right," Rebecca sounded excited. "You can cover up the mistakes with icing..."

"And you could put silver sparkles on it," Mia added.

I began to feel a little bit excited myself. I ran to the cupboard and found a huge bag of icing sugar. There was a box of little silver balls as well, and I fetched those too. My friends helped me mix the icing and get it exactly the right colour – and by the time I'd finished even I was pleased. It looked EXACTLY like the bow on Fairy Angora's dress – only more sparkly!

"It looks absolutely brilliant!" Lindsey clapped her hands. "Fairy Angora's going to love it!"

The bell went for bedtime as we finished clearing up. We left the cake on the table in the cookery room, and made our way along the corridor to the dormitories. Diamonde and Gruella had left the door of their dormitory wide open, and we couldn't help seeing

the dresses hanging by their beds...and we STARED! They were EXACTLY the same as the dress Duchess Delia had made for Fairy Angora...except that these dresses were pink.

"WOW!" Caitlin's eyes were as round as saucers.

"They've even got hooped petticoats," Lindsey said.

Anna folded her arms. "Do you think we should tell Fairy G?"

"We can't," Abigail told her. "We shouldn't have looked through the door."

That was true, so we hurried on to Tulip Room...but as we got ready for bed we couldn't help wondering what Fairy Angora would think. And as I was drifting off to sleep I thought of something else. How would Diamonde get inside her cake? The dresses had hoops...she'd never fit!

Chapter Four

I had forgotten all about Diamonde and Gruella and their dresses when I woke up the next morning. The bell went extra early, and we rushed down to breakfast in our dressing gowns. Fairy G had told us we weren't to get dressed until breakfast was over. We could see the pavilion in the rose garden from the dining room window, and it looked magnificent. There was even a rose-coloured flag flying from the top!

Then it was time to go and get dressed – and that was SUCH fun! Fairy G came stomping in soon afterwards to tell us we were to be ready by the front door in ten minutes time.

"Be careful," she warned. "There are hundreds of carriages and coaches rolling up the drive. All Fairy Angora's friends are coming."

I suddenly thought of something. "Please," I said, "when should we fetch our cake? It's still in the cookery room."

"I've already thought of that," Fairy G told me. "I've sent one page to fetch your cake, and another to fetch Diamonde and Gruella's." She raised an eyebrow. "They're being very mysterious. Do you know what their cake looks like?"

We told her we'd been sworn to secrecy, and she laughed her booming laugh. We laughed too, and we almost danced our way to the front door where our baskets of roses were waiting for us. We picked them up and got into pairs. I was walking beside Lindsey, and I was pleased, because she never gets worried about things like I do.

When Fairy Angora came down the steps we gasped. She looked SO beautiful, and her dress was glorious. Then Queen Mother Matilda appeared and told us to start walking...and it seemed no time at all before we'd reached

the pavilion. Fairy Angora took her place on the stage, and we began to toss our rose petals into the air – and the most wonderful thing happened. The rose petals swirled round and round... and drifted to the floor to make the prettiest rose petal carpet.

I saw Fairy G looking suspiciously twinkly as King Percy stood up and made his speech, and I was almost certain she'd been using her wand. Then came a massive fanfare of trumpets. Fairy G stepped forward, and handed Fairy Angora her Final Certificate.

We clapped as loudly as we could, and so did all the princesses and fairies in the audience. The applause went on and on; Fairy Angora blushed very pink and curtsied again and again, and finally Fairy G held up her hand.

"Dear Fairy Angora – two of our princesses have something for you," she said, and waved her hand at the pavilion entrance. The curtains swung open, and Diamonde and Gruella swept towards the stage...and they were carrying OUR cake!

Fairy Angora looked thrilled to bits. "OH!" she gasped, "OH! Thank you, Diamonde! Thank you, Gruella! It's the most wonderful cake I've ever seen! And to copy the bow from my dress – that's so thoughtful!"

I could hardly breathe. I couldn't spoil Fairy Angora's day by accusing the twins of stealing my cake, but I was SO shocked and disappointed...and then I saw Fairy G staring at me.

She looked very thoughtful.
I swallowed, and turned away in
case she saw the tears in my eyes.

King Percy was beaming.
"Excellent work, princesses," he
said. "I'm delighted. Really, really
delighted. Perhaps you would like

to sit with Fairy Angora for the
Rose Petal Picnic?"

Gruella simpered. "We'd be
pleased to," she said, "but first
we've got a poem for Fairy
Angora." She fished in her bag,
and brought out a piece of paper.

"Fairy Angora,
this is your special day,
So we've popped out of a cake
to say 'Hooray!'
And we think you are very clever,
And we hope you are a good fairy
Godmother for ever and ever."

"Thank you, Princess Gruella," Fairy G said. "Now, before we begin the picnic, the princesses from Tulip Room have one last surprise." She pointed to the entrance of the pavilion. I saw a page step out wheeling Diamonde and Gruella's enormous cake in front of him...

...and the cake was in pieces.

I knew exactly what had happened. Diamonde had tried to get inside, but her hooped petticoats had meant she was too big...and that was why she and Gruella had taken our cake. And now we were left with a mess, but there was nothing we could do about it. What would we say?

Chapter Five

Everyone turned to look, and for a moment there was a murmur as if they were shocked...but then it changed into a murmur of astonishment. As the page pushed the cake towards the stage the air filled with sparkles, the cake shook itself...and it was whole again! Fairy G gave a little chuckle, and handed Fairy Angora a silver knife. "Do please cut the cake."

"It's almost too beautiful to cut," Fairy Angora said, but she took the knife and cut the cake open...

And six snow white doves flew out! They were carrying a garland of roses in their beaks and, as everyone gazed at them in amazement, they flew to Fairy Angora and draped it round her shoulders.

"OH!" she gasped. "I thought the last cake was wonderful, but this is...oh, it's too lovely for words!"

Fairy G lifted up her hand. "Gruella dear," she said quietly. "Could you read us your poem again?"

Gruella looked surprised, but she pulled the poem out of her bag for the second time.

Fairy Angora,
this is your special day
So we've popped out of a cake
to say 'Hooray'..."

She put her hand to her mouth. "Oh," she said. "Oh. I was meant to say, 'Popped up WITH a cake...'"

Diamonde turned on her sister.

"Gruella! You ALWAYS ruin EVERYTHING!" she shouted, and then she ran out of the pavilion.

Gruella gulped, and ran after her.

There was complete silence as everyone realised something had gone very wrong. But then Fairy G waved her wand...and more sparkles flew everywhere. There

was the sound of tinkling bells, and a wonderful scent of roses...and as it faded away I knew that nobody in the audience would remember what Gruella and Diamonde had done.

Instead they came hurrying to congratulate Fairy Angora, and to tell us how special the cakes were, and to say what fun it had been seeing the doves fly out.

All Fairy G said was that there had been a mix up. "Tulip Room are such Perfect Princesses," she said. "They said nothing when Princess Diamonde and Princess Gruella brought out the wrong cake." She gave us such a beaming smile that I felt as if I had a warm glow inside me. "They are truly wonderful."

King Percy came over to thank us very much, but then he disappeared as soon as we made our way to the tables for the picnic. I almost – but not quite – felt sorry for Diamonde and Gruella as he marched off to find them with a grim look on his face. I didn't have time to worry, though, because the picnic was SO fantastic. The fairies said SUCH nice things, and

I think Fairy G must have
waved her magic wand over the
rose-flavoured chocolate creams
because they never ran out...
even though she ate hundreds!

And when the dancing began it
was glorious...

...and we danced and we danced until the stars came out.

Fairy G and Fairy Angora were still dancing as we made our way to Tulip Room and Fairy Angora looked SO happy.

Chapter Six

That night when we were sitting up in bed Bethany said, "I think that was the most wonderful day of my whole life."

"But it could easily have been the very WORST day," Rebecca pointed out.

"Wasn't it brilliant when the cake mended itself?" Mia said dreamily.

"How did Fairy G know what had happened?"

Caitlin smiled. "I'd say she guessed as soon as Gruella said that silly poem."

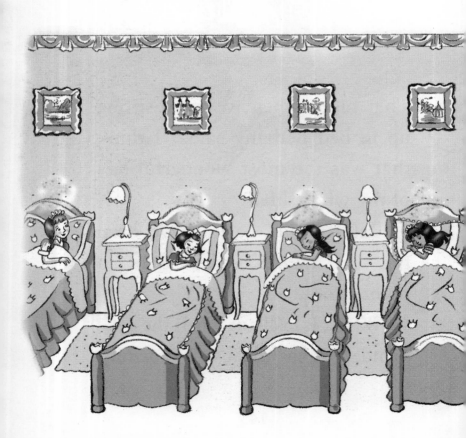

I giggled. "I think she must have seen the look on my face when they brought in our cake."

"You did look just a little bit like a goldfish," Anna told me.

But I didn't mind. I was with my sister and all my friends, and that's the best place to be in the whole wide world...

...and I'm so SO glad that you're here too.

Enjoy more fabulous Tiara Club adventures!

ISBN 978 1 40830 582 9

£4.99

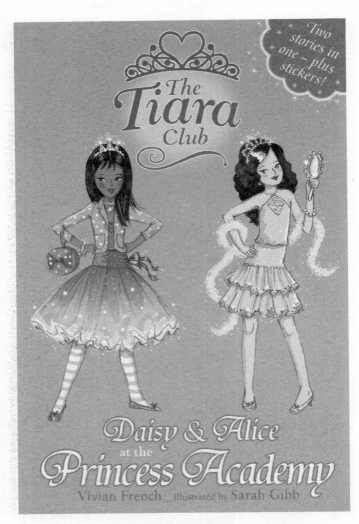

Two stories in one – plus stickers!

The Tiara Club

Daisy & Alice at the Princess Academy

Vivian French   Illustrated by Sarah Gibb

ISBN 978 1 40830 583 6

£4.99

Two stories in one – plus stickers!

The Tiara Club

Sophia & Emily
at the
Princess Academy

Vivian French   Illustrated by Sarah Gibb

ISBN 978 1 40830 584 3

£4.99

The Tiara Club

Two stories in one – plus stickers!

Charlotte & Katie
at
Silver Towers

Vivian French   Illustrated by Sarah Gibb

ISBN 978 1 40830 675 8

£4.99

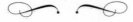

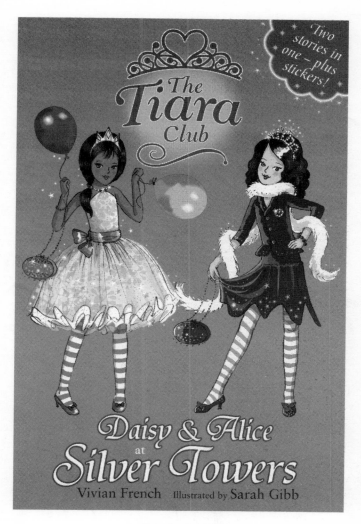

Two stories in one – plus stickers!

The Tiara Club

Daisy & Alice at Silver Towers

Vivian French   Illustrated by Sarah Gibb

ISBN 978 1 40830 676 5

£4.99

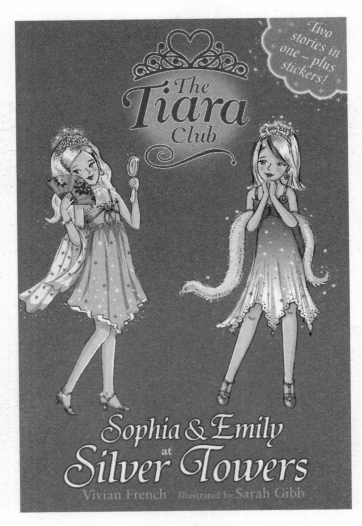

Two stories in one – plus stickers!

The Tiara Club

Sophia & Emily at Silver Towers

Vivian French   Illustrated by Sarah Gibb

ISBN 978 1 40830 677 2

£4.99

Have you read the Tiara Club at Ruby Mansions?

ISBN 978 1 84616 290 9

£3.99

ISBN 978 1 84616 291 6

£3.99

ISBN 978 1 84616 292 3

£3.99

ISBN 978 1 84616 293 0

£3.99

ISBN 978 1 84616 294 7

£3.99

ISBN 978 1 84616 295 4

£3.99

Have you read the Tiara Club at Pearl Palace?

ISBN 978 1 84616 498 9

£3.99

ISBN 978 1 84616 499 6

£3.99

ISBN 978 1 84616 500 9

£3.99

ISBN 978 1 84616 501 6

£3.99

ISBN 978 1 84616 502 3

£3.99

ISBN 978 1 84616 503 0

£3.99

Have you read the Tiara Club at Emerald Castle?

ISBN 978 1 84616 869 7

£3.99

ISBN 978 1 84616 870 3

£3.99

ISBN 978 1 84616 871 0

£3.99

ISBN 978 1 84616 872 7

£3.99

ISBN 978 1 84616 873 4

£3.99

ISBN 978 1 84616 874 1

£3.99

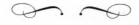

Have you read the Tiara Club
at Diamond Turrets?

ISBN 978 1 84616 875 8

£3.99

ISBN 978 1 84616 876 5

£3.99

ISBN 978 1 84616 877 2

£3.99

ISBN 978 1 84616 878 9

£3.99

ISBN 978 1 84616 879 6

£3.99

ISBN 978 1 84616 880 2

£3.99

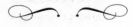

Have you read the Tiara Club specials?

ISBN 978 1 84616 296 1

£5.99

ISBN 978 1 84616 470 5

£5.99

ISBN 978 1 84616 504 7

£5.99

ISBN 978 1 84616 881 9

£5.99

ISBN 978 1 84616 882 6

£5.99

ISBN 978 1 40830 579 9

£5.99

ISBN 978 1 40830 580 5

£5.99

Don't miss  The **Tiara** Club website at:

www.tiaraclub.co.uk

Keep up to date with the latest
Tiara Club books and meet all
your favourite princesses!

There is SO much to see and do,
including games and activities. You can
even become an exclusive member of the
Tiara Club Princess Academy.

PLUS, there's exciting
competitions with
WONDERFUL prizes!

Be a Perfect Princess — check it out today!